The Wristwatch

PRAISE FOR *STORYSHARES*

"One of the brightest innovators and game-changers in the education industry."
– Forbes

"Your success in applying research-validated practices to promote literacy serves as a valuable model for other organizations seeking to create evidence-based literacy programs."

- Library of Congress

"We need powerful social and educational innovation, and Storyshares is breaking new ground. The organization addresses critical problems facing our students and teachers. I am excited about the strategies it brings to the collective work of making sure every student has an equal chance in life."
– Teach For America

"Around the world, this is one of the up-and-coming trailblazers changing the landscape of literacy and education."
- International Literacy Association

"It's the perfect idea. There's really nothing like this. I mean wow, this will be a wonderful experience for young people."   - Andrea Davis Pinkney, Executive Director, Scholastic

"Reading for meaning opens opportunities for a lifetime of learning. Providing emerging readers with engaging texts that are designed to offer both challenges and support for each individual will improve their lives for years to come. Storyshares is a wonderful start."
- David Rose, Co-founder of CAST & UDL

The Wristwatch

Elizabeth Ludlam

STORYSHARES

Story Share, Inc.
New York. Boston. Philadelphia.

Published in the United States by Story Share, Inc.

Storyshares
Story Share, Inc.
24 N. Bryn Mawr Avenue #340
Bryn Mawr, PA 19010-3304
www.storyshares.org

Inspiring reading with a new kind of book.

Interest Level: High School
Grade Level Equivalent: 4.3

9781642612134

Book design by Storyshares

Printed in the United States of America

Storyshares Presents

1

Jessica glanced down at her wristwatch. It was a pretty thing, with a white, heart-shaped face surrounded by blood-red rubies. A thin gold band secured it to her delicate wrist. Her mother had given it to her two years ago on her fourteenth birthday. It was the only piece of jewelry she owned, and she treasured it dearly.

In fact, besides the one dress she was expected to wear when she appeared in public, it was the only thing of value she had owned since her parents had died in a carriage accident. Her Great Aunt Genevieve had consented to take Jessica in only after five orphanages and one alcoholic cousin all refused to take her. She had snatched up all of Jessica's valuable belongings, along with the sizable inheritance her parents had left her. Jessica had managed to hide the watch from her aunt. Now she only wore it when she was all alone, locked up in her dark, dingy bedroom.

2

At this moment, her watch told her it was exactly six-forty in the morning. *Twenty more minutes*, Jessica thought, biting her lip. She didn't think she could wait that long.

She glanced at her reflection in the dusty, cracked mirror propped against a beaten-up copy of Oliver Twist that sat on her otherwise empty desk.

Two years ago, she had been a beautiful young lady with long, golden curls that bounced when she walked, clear blue eyes, rosy cheeks, and a creamy complexion. Her mother always said that, because of both her looks and her fortune, she could have any husband she wanted. Now, however, Jessica was not so sure. Thanks to Great Aunt Genevieve, her fortune had vanished along with the happy life she had lived with her parents.

Staring into the mirror, she wondered if her mother would even recognize her. The pretty fourteen-year-old was long gone. In her place stood a tall and gangly sixteen-year-old. Two years of being locked up in her bedroom with little to eat had left her skinny and sickly pale. Her bones jutted out awkwardly, and her once beautiful hair had become a dull, tangled mess. Her eyes were sunken and her lips were thin. You could tell by looking at her that she had not smiled in a very long time.

3

Jessica checked her watch again. Sixteen more minutes.

She paced back and forth, chewing her lip. The back of her right thigh ached where Great Aunt Genevieve had smacked her leg with her cane yesterday. Sometimes, Jessica thought the old woman had made a sport of whacking her with that cane.

Thirteen more minutes. Jessica was growing anxious. What if something went wrong? No, that was not possible. She had made sure that everything would go as planned.

She kept pacing. Her feet were cold. She wished that Great Aunt Genevieve had given her a pair of slippers for Christmas instead of the cracked mirror. She often wondered if her aunt had given her that mirror just so she could have a daily reminder of how ugly she had become.

She glanced down at her wrist. Nine more minutes.

4

She could hear her heart beating inside her chest. Outside, she heard the sound of a bird singing. It was such a beautiful sound. It reminded Jessica of how her mother used to play the piano and sing at night, before bedtime.

Her mother had the most wonderful voice, like the sweet flow of honey. When she sang, the entire world stopped to listen. The crickets ceased their chirping, the dogs ceased their barking, the children ceased their laughing, the wolves ceased their howling, all to listen to her mother's song.

Jessica smiled at the memory. It had been so long since she had heard the sound of music. Great Aunt Genevieve detested music of any sort. She said it hurt her ears and it was not lady-like for a girl listen to songs.

Five more minutes. Soon now. Very soon.

Jessica stopped pacing and sat down on the edge of her bed. The lumpy mattress creaked. Once, Jessica remembered, as a punishment for dripping soup on her dress during dinner when Great Aunt Genevieve's friend was visiting, her bed was taken away for two weeks. She had been forced to sleep on the cold, hard floor. Needless to say, Jessica did not get much sleep those two weeks.

Her watch ticked. Three more minutes.

5

She bit her lip hard until she tasted blood. She wiped her mouth with the back of her hand and glanced down to see a dark red streak across her skin. Her stomach lurched at the sight, although she should be used to it by now. How many times had Jessica been bloodied and bruised by her great aunt's awful cane? How many times had the maid, Nicole, stitched up gashes in Jessica's skin and wiped the blood from her wounds?

Jessica felt a twinge of guilt in her heart at the thought of Nicole, the only person who had ever treated her with kindness in the past two years. It was too late, however, to spare Nicole. The deed was done. There was no turning back.

Two more minutes. The pounding of Jessica's heart seemed to synchronize with the sound of her watch ticking.

One more minute. Outside her door, Jessica heard the sound of Nicole's footsteps as she made her routine trip up the stairs to wake Great Aunt Genevieve from her slumber.

Thirty seconds. The stairs creaked loudly.

Fifteen seconds. She bit her lip even harder.

Five... Four... Three... Two... One...

6

For the longest moment, there was only silence. Then she heard it. The strangled wail of the maid. She listened calmly as Nicole ran, sobbing, from Great Aunt Genevieve's room. And then, in a voice louder than Jessica thought could come out of frail little Nicole's lungs, she yelled, "Ms. Genevieve is dead!"

Jessica smiled, just a little. And in a quiet voice, she whispered, "I know."

The Wristwatch

About The Author

Elizabeth Ludlam is a contributing author to the Storyshares library.

About The Publisher

Story Shares is a nonprofit focused on supporting the millions of teens and adults who struggle with reading by creating a new shelf in the library specifically for them. The ever-growing collection features content that is compelling and culturally relevant for teens and adults, yet still readable at a range of lower reading levels.

Story Shares generates content by engaging deeply with writers, bringing together a community to create this new kind of book. With more intriguing and approachable stories to choose from, the teens and adults who have fallen behind are improving their skills and beginning to discover the joy of reading. For more information, visit storyshares.org.

Easy to Read. Hard to Put Down.